Little
ANXIOUS
Cat

sounds true
BOULDER, COLORADO

Little
ANXIOUS
Cat

Audrey Bouquet
Fabien Öckto Lambert

a BiG
EMOTIONS
BOOK

Little Cat is feeling fine.

But when he finds out he needs
to go to the doctor for a checkup,
he doesn't feel so fine anymore.

His dad shows him his health record.
Today the doctor will just weigh and measure him.
He won't have to get any shots.

But Little Cat doesn't want to go.

In the waiting room, his heart is racing. He has
a sore throat and a tummy ache. Everything in
his little body freezes up. Even his dad's hugs
can't keep him from crying.

Here's the doctor now.
He takes one look at Little Cat
and can see right away how
anxious he is to be there.

L W F P

Z G O M s

The doctor is very reassuring.
He tells Little Cat he's going to
use his anti-stress superpowers.
He asks Little Cat to do what he does.
"Wow!" Little Cat thinks.

The doctor starts to jump up and down,
swinging his arms like a rag doll.

Little Cat does exactly what the doctor does. He starts to laugh. And just like magic, he feels more relaxed.

Then the doctor and Little Cat count mice together.

LA RESPIRATION

1	
2	
3	
4	

1 mouse, deep breath in.

2 mice, deep breath out.

3 mice, deep breath in.

4 mice, deep breath out.

Now Little Cat's breathing feels easy, and his heart beats gently.

Next, the doctor asks Little Cat
to think of his favorite superhero.
Little Cat closes his eyes and imagines
himself in a magic cape and boots.

Now, he can be brave too!

All the nervous-tummy butterflies have flown away.

He's ready to be examined, measured, and weighed.

Little Cat is feeling just fine now. And next time when he comes back for his shot, he'll use his superpowers to conquer his anxiety.

Sounds True
Boulder, CO 80306

Text © 2022 Audrey Bouquet
Illustrations © 2022 Fabien Öckto Lambert
Translated from the French by Margot Kerlidou and Alyson Waters

Published 2022

Book & cover design by Ranée Kahler
Cover illustration by Fabien Öckto Lambert

Printed in South Korea

Library of Congress Cataloging-in-Publication Data

Names: Bouquet, Audrey, author. | Kerlidou, Margot, translator. |
    Waters, Alyson, 1955- translator. | Öckto Lambert, Fabien, 1985-illustrator.
Title: Little anxious Cat / by Audrey Bouquet ; illustrated by
    Fabien Öckto Lambert; translated from the French by Margot Kerlidou
    and Alyson Waters.
Other titles: Émotions de petit chat anxieux. English
Description: Boulder, CO : Sounds True, 2022. | Series: A big emotions book |
    "Originally published as Les émotions de Petit Chat anxieux in 2019." |
    Audience: Ages 2-5. | Summary: Little Cat is nervous to visit the
    doctor and learns ways to relax so he can let go of his anxiety.
Identifiers: LCCN 2021036482 | ISBN 9781683648376 (hardback)
Subjects: CYAC: Cats--Fiction. | Anxiety--Fiction. | Medical care--Fiction. |
    LCGFT: Picture books.
Classification: LCC PZ7.1.B6815 Li 2022 | DDC [E]--dc23
LC record available at https://lccn.loc.gov/2021036482

10 9 8 7 6 5 4 3 2 1